ISBN 0-590-45409-9

Text copyright © 1991 by Bill Martin Jr.
Illustrations copyright © 1991 by Eric Carle.
All rights reserved. Published by Scholastic Inc.,
730 Broadway, New York, NY 10003, by arrangement with
Henry Holt and Company, Inc.

12 11 10 9 8 7 6 5 4 3 2 1   2 3 4 5 6 7/9

Printed in the U.S.A.

First Scholastic printing, September 1992

Polar Bear, Polar Bear, What Do You Hear?

By Bill Martin Jr
Pictures by Eric Carle

SCHOLASTIC BOOK CLUB EDITION

Polar Bear, Polar Bear,
what do you hear?

I hear a lion
roaring in my ear.

Lion, Lion,
what do you hear?

I hear a hippopotamus
snorting in my ear.

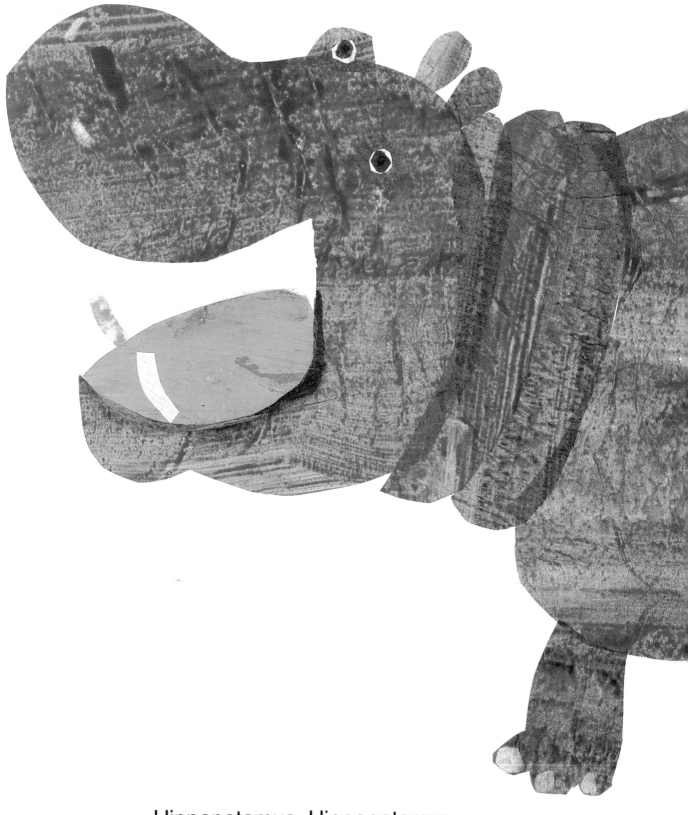

Hippopotamus, Hippopotamus,
what do you hear?

I hear a flamingo
fluting in my ear.

Flamingo, Flamingo,
what do you hear?

I hear a zebra
braying in my ear.

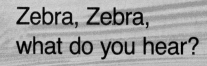

Zebra, Zebra,
what do you hear?

I hear a boa constrictor
hissing in my ear.

Boa Constrictor, Boa Constrictor,
what do you hear?

I hear an elephant
trumpeting in my ear.

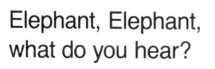

Elephant, Elephant,
what do you hear?

I hear a leopard
snarling in my ear.

Leopard, Leopard,
what do you hear?

I hear a peacock
yelping in my ear.

Peacock, Peacock,
what do you hear?

I hear a walrus
bellowing in my ear.

Walrus, Walrus,
what do you hear?

I hear a zookeeper
whistling in my ear.

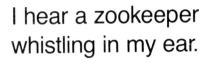

Zookeeper, Zookeeper,
what do you hear?

I hear children . . .

. . . growling like a polar bear,
roaring like a lion,
snorting like a hippopotamus,
fluting like a flamingo,
braying like a zebra,
hissing like a boa constrictor,
trumpeting like an elephant,
snarling like a leopard,
yelping like a peacock,
bellowing like a walrus . . .

that's what I hear.